John Allyn, Robert Treat, William Pitkin

Their Majesties Colony of Connecticut in New-England

Vindicated

from the abuses of a pamphlet, licensed and printed at New-York 1694 :

Intituled, Some seasonable considerations for the good people of

Connecticut

John Allyn, Robert Treat, William Pitkin

Their Majesties Colony of Connecticut in New-England Vindicated
from the abuses of a pamphlet, licensed and printed at New-York 1694 : Intituled,
Some seasonable considerations for the good people of Connecticut

ISBN/EAN: 9783337250881

Printed in Europe, USA, Canada, Australia, Japan

Cover: Foto ©Andreas Hilbeck / pixelio.de

More available books at **www.hansebooks.com**

Their Majesties COLONY

OF

CONNECTICUT

in New-England

VINDICATED,

From the Abuses

Of a Pamphlet, Licensed and printed at *New-York* 1694.
Intituled,
Some Seasonable Considerations for the Good People of Connecticut.

By an Answer Thereunto.

Exod. 22. 28. *Thou shalt not Raile upon the Judges; neither Speak Evil of the Ruler of thy People.*

Prov. 10. 18. *He that Dissembleth Hatred with Lying Lips, and he that Inventeth a Slander is a Fool.*

Prov. 14. 3. *In the mouth of the Foolish is the Rod of Pride: but the Lips of the wise preserve them.*

BOSTON in NEW-ENGLAND.

Printed by *Bartholomew Green*. Anno Dom. 1694.

Hartford, April. 23d. 1694.

THE Governour and Assistants met, do Order this Answer to the Pamphlet Intituled, [*Some Seasonable Considerations for the Good People of Connecticut*] to be forthwith Printed.

ROBERT TREAT, *Governour.*
JOHN ALLYN, *Secretary.*

To the READER.

COURTEOUS READER,

THIS *small Tract, must chiefly own its Perusal; To thy willingness to hear an Asperssed People* (and Their Majesties Subjects) *Vindicated, from almost Unparraled Abuses. We were necessitated to its Publication, by a* Pamphlet *written* (as it is intimated in it) *by one of this Colony of* Connecticut: *and Licensed and Printed at* New-York *in the present Year* 1694. *Which being spread abroad into the World, and so also will lye to Posterity to our Defamation. It was thought our Duty & Interest to give it an Answer; and not by Silence to be Accessory to our own* (so great) *Wrongs: Let the Candid* Reader *Consider the Wise Mans Intimation,* That in the Answering of some men there is a sort of being like them inevitable. *Wherefore we Advertise, That the Real or seeming Harshness of our Answer, is not in Revenge but for our* Just *Defence & Vindication. To the Remedy of a Cancerous Humour something* (yea much) *of a Proportionable Accrimony ought to be allowed; what thereby of Reproof falls on our Impeachers is Accidental, to our endeavour. We have not departed from Truth, Shuned any thing of Strength, nor misrepresented him whom we answer; in any thing we know of:* and as the Reader, *if he hath that* Pamphlet *may find: We were put upon what we have herein done by the call of some highly concerned for the* Colony, *as well as the Occasion it self given. Our plain way* (in this able & curious Age) *of Writting, has no Apology, but what the kind* Reader *will make for men, who have so little Occasion as we have to improve the* PRESS. *Some may think we complain too much: let the Occasion be Consid-*

ered, *and it may be seen that our Stroke is heavier than our Groaning,* Job 23. 2. *To those that have Injured us by that* Book, *we would wish them no worse than* Repentance *of it, and* Pardon *for it.* The Lord is Righteous in all this & other Evils that have come on us, for we have Sinned against Him. *J. A. W. P.*

An Answer to A

PAMPHLET,

Intituled,

"Some Seasonable Considerations for the Good people of
"Connecticut,   *Printed at New-York,* 1694.

IT becomes an Honest Writer, to introduce his Book into
the World, with a Title fitting the Scope and Intend-
ment of it: But whosoever hath Perused this we are answering would rather have thought, such a Title as this,
Proper to it:
  Viz.

1. Unreasonable Essayes, to Represent *Connecticut* to be
Inconsiderate, Irreligious, Rebelious *&c.* or something
Equivalent; which is the Argument of the Book, as is but
too manifest by it. Whither under this Pretence of *Seasonable Advice* there be not the greatest Violence and Injury,
offered to the Reputation, and Interest of *Connecticut:* will
be in part seen, by what we have to say on this account.
We would Unmask it therefore, only with this intimation
here, that another thing than *Seasonable Advice* to us, is intended, and prosecuted in that Piece.

[6]   2. As to its Seasonableness: It is evidently otherwise; the cause therein Agitated, depending now before
Their Majesties, and not Issuable by a *Pamphleters* Advice;
which is wholly disproportionate to that concern: yet indeed in some respects, it may be very Seasonable: namely,
to stir Factions (though it hath missed that too as yet) and
to make us odious to the World (which seems to be mainly
intended in it) and to prejudice our cause (which he that
Wrote might have been too late, for had he staied the Result)

in *England;* and if Occasion serve, for after Severities; this is a Seasonable fore-condemning of us: If these, and the like, make it Seasonable, and Suiting its writers, and Licensers designs upon us, Seasonable it is. But it may appear, that the whole work in its design and management hath little of Justice or Charity, whatever it hath of the contrary.

3. The Epithet of Good People, he gives here; he utterly takes away, and contradicts all along after; the kindness of it here therefore is worthy no notice, but onely, that in his Title he begins not Sincerely.

We must come to the work it self: he saith,

PAMPHLET. *Advice was given us in the Year* 1689. *when we were about to make our Revolution* (as tis called) *and for ought I know, it had been good for us that we had taken it.*

ANSWER. 1. By what is most probable? he that gave that Advice, dwells not far from him that gives these aleadged Seasonable Considerations: and is but his own Patron and commender here.

2. That Advice is well enough known, to have been given in the other Colonies, as well as here: the substance of it was; to manage the Government (by Commissions granted by Sir. *Edmund Andross*) after the Revolution made at *Boston;* and to decline Charters.

3. This Advice was not followed in *Massachusetts, Plymouth, Rhoad-Island,* no, nor *York*, the Reasons have formerly been Rendred: we think to the Satisfaction of all, but only the Irreconcileable Enemies of Charter Government, which is so well known to be dear to the People of *New England*.

[7] PAMPHLET. *But we are so unwilling to be Advised, and so ill Affected to any, that tell us the truth, that there is little Incouragement, to any to Expose themselves in that kind for the future.*

ANSWER. 1. Unless this Person would be attended, as the only Oracle of *New England;* and impose on all other mens understandings and Consciences: there is little Reason for him thus Complainingly to charge the body of the People, with being unwiling to be Advised: and being ill affected, to any that tell us the truth; his notions were considered and advised on largely. But other Reasons did preponderate, in the Judgment of the most, in a manner of all: as is well known.

2. The Publick accounts given by the Reverend Mr. *Mather*, of His Majesties Approbation, of that Revolution at *Boston;* with a now above five years implicite allowance off the measures here taken, might have taken of the fondness here paid to that advice. But some Counselers, if not attended will be angry [so was *Achittophel*] and seek revenge some where.

PAMPHLET. And it is he sayes, *An Evil time, and the Prudent shall keep Silence—Cast not your Pearls before Swine &c.*

ANSWER. 1. Its great Pitty he did not keep Silence, or speak better: but if he follow not his own Advice, it will impede others to follow it.

2. It is not over modest to Emblazon his own Advices, thus as Pearles; and how unworthy this his Composure, is of such a Representation! will not be difficult to an Impartial Reader, to Judge of.

3. To compare a *Colony*, to harmful *Swine*, is hard, and yet harder; when if we be so, in respect of the Advice in 1689. in a manner all the People of *New-England* are so. But such a whole Sale Champman, that thus Barters all our Credite; will deserve an Examination.

4. Here begins, what is carried on all along his Book: namely, a misapplication of Holy Scripture. Whether this be not a great Prophaning the Holy Name of GOD, is [8] more meet for others to ‖ Consider; than for us here to say. What? are his Advices to be Similized with the truths of the Gospel? which are the *Pearls* there spoken of: or is *New-Englands* not attending those things from him, and others of his Opinion; to be represented and made abominable, by the fellest Persecution against the

Gospel? The Excesses of this kind, and the Rating and Blemishing (if not Curssing us) by the mouth of Scripture; are no small Scandal to us; and we desire it may be well considered by the Pious Readers.

But this notwithstanding, he proceeds to tell us;

PAMPHLET. *That he hopes the case is not so desperate.*

ANSWER. We hope so too, yet he all along, gives us up as in the most desperate hopeless posture.

PAMPHLET. He then pleads it his duty; *Thou shalt not hate thy Brother in thy heart, but shall Rebuke him &c.*

ANSWER. If any can reasonably judge, that more of hatred, and less of Love could be exerted, by the *Pamphleter*, than is to be found in him here: they may believe he hath performed this, as his duty. But we may not dwell on every Particular. Let it be noted that the Scripture here aleadged as a warrant to this Book, is *Levit* 19. 17. and the verse next before it, *Viz.* 16. is, *Thou shalt not walk about with Tales among thy People ; thou shalt not stand against the Blood of thy Neighbour, I am the Lord.* Which seems as full and direct a prohibition of this his work as readily can be found in the *Bible.*

2. Having thus Prefaced himself; our Adviser or rather judge; and *Connecticut* People the Objects of his pleasure : in the Second place, in *Page 1st. 2d.* He calls to a Serious Attention, by *Scriptures* and *Arguments*, no less weighty, than his Occasion and use of them are Slighty ; as will appear, we need not transcribe him.

ANSWER. All the things he proposes (that are true) are Obvious, and have been considered, and needed not his Repetition.

2. *This* (like many other things) is a Representing us to the World; as Ignorant and Inconsiderate to an Excess. [9] But these ‖ Artifices, every candid Reader will easily detect; to whom we refer it to consider, whether the following things in that *Pamphlet,* be adapted to our Advice and consideration ; or to Breath out his own Spirit against

us, and to furnish ill minded men, with matter and words, to defame us; to ensnare the more unwary, into hard thoughts; and many into groundless fears.

3. His Prefacing thus ended, in *Page* 3. He tells of the Commission of *Leiutenancy* over the *Militia* of this *Colony;* His Excellency Sir. *William Phipps* had : and saith :

PAMPHLET. *But upon notice hereof, a General Assembly was called, and met, and there it was Resolved: Not to submit to it, nor to take any notice of* Sir. William Phipps *in that capacity.*

ANS. 1. That His Excellency Sir. *William Phipps*, in His Commission had such a *Leiutenancy* Granted by Their Majesties and that the General Court met, is true.

2. That His Excellency did give an account of it, and desired to know what Officers were in Commission, and at length sent a Copy of that His Commission, is also true.

3. That the General Court, at their meeting did send His Excellency an account, what our intentions were, as to Addressing Their Majesties, in that behalf; and that in the Interim, the *Military Officers*, were to good Satisfaction, is also true.

4. As to the Resolve of the Court, here asserted : We say these things. (1.) That it seems to be of absolute necessity, to the ends of the *Pamphlet*, to charge such Resolves, and Acts of the Court, upon them with Rising in Arms &c. Else, they could not make out, Opposing Their Majesties, and so lay a foundation large enough, to Superstruct all the revilings and menaces, that for the ends he had before him, must be used. (2.) If such a Resolve were, our Governour, who was then in Court, must put the Question, which it did Resolve, and this is an high Reflection on him. (3.) Since this *Pamphlet* was *Licensed* at *York*, and things of this nature Asserted in it; it behoved in Justice, that he had Attested Copies, or other Equivalent assurance of it ere he thus expose us. (4.) We love not such course words as to tell the World that what is so

said, is an absolute Lye: and yet this we must say (if we [10] will say the truth) for there was no such Question ‖ *put*, nor no such Resolve made; and we challenge them to prove it, that say it: and who that finds such things, so certified, and hears no other, would doubt the truth of it; or demurr to conclude us Direct Opposers of Their Majesties. But we have more of this kind, to come in yet, wherein an amazing, Impudent Falsifying, is used against us. (5.) It will not heal the evil to make a *Subterfuge* of any inferences from other things, as arguing such a Resolve: for 'tis matter of Fact, that is here asserted, and not brought in as a Consequence of what was matter of Fact: for that had been but Opinion; whereas this is Exhibited, as a Court Act, or Resolve.

PAM. He saies further, *At another General Assembly, we resolve to Address Their Majesties forthwith*—(and) *yet no Address is made to Their Majesties.*

ANS. It is not true to say no Address is made, we did forthwith, with all possible diligence, send our Address: that we have no account of it, is from other causes than our not sending. It is a very sad thing thus openly to be rendred as meer dissemblers, with Sir. *William*, and Their Majesties Especially: but this is the measure that is mete us, and surely Mr. *Clarkson* gave his *Imprimatur* on very fallible grounds to this.

PAM. *After which, Sir.* William Phipps *making some further demands in the* Spring 1693. *we promised to pay him some Hundreds of Pounds, and to take upon us the defence of the upper Towns, upon the River, belonging to the* Massachusetts. *As if these things would Satisfy Their Majesties Commission?* (and these things, in *Page* 6.) he calleth a *Composition* with Sir. *William Phipps*, which gives his meaning, and what he would suggest, and have believed in the World, as to the Transactions between His Excellency, and this *Colony.*

ANS. 1. He that hath only this *Pamphlets* information in this, and Credits it, will be tempted to think: that those

Hundreds of Pounds were a *Bribe*, engaged and accepted. This is an Affront to His Excellency as well as to us, to Represent a thing after this manner, which was in some sort true.

2. The truth was, in Effect only this: *His Excellency designing to disrest the Enemy* Indians, *at the* Eastward, *sent to* [11] *us for men to Aid* ‖ *therein; and because we could not (without great inconvenience) send men so far (by two* Gentlemen *that were sent down on purpose) we tendred* 400. Pound, *for furthering that Expedition, if it went on as was propounded: but not a Penny to compound with him, about his Commission, as* · *the* Pamphlet *would insinuate: and the offer was made openly to His* Excellencies Council; *not secretly to His* Excellency: *and which was done sincerely for Their* Majesties *Service: and we must complain of this partial account, and Representation of the* Pamphlets; *as setting a false face on, and misconstruing that Action.*

3. We undertook not absolutely, the defence of the upper *Towns;* but only to such a number of men, as occasion should be: which was accordingly performed, to our no small charge: but to an envious eye, will pervert the best actions, in accounting them to the World for what they never were.

4. Here we must remark, the observable difference, between the Treatment we had with His *Excellency* and the *Gent.* of *Boston*, and what we now have from this writer, on these Occasions. We may believe, that they had as more to do with it, so as much Integrity and Prudence, to manage such a thing with us, and much more, than this medler, yet never handled it as he has done.

5. Notwithstanding this seeming care for this first Commission, it is to be noted, that in all the time of it, our Adversary never gave us any such *Seasonable Advice*, to comply with it, as now, in a Month (as it is intimated in *Page* 7.) he is all on a light fire against us, why were not the dangers of delaying, and addressing, then set before us; since

himself saith, *that sincere Obedience is Universal.* So would his to Their Majesties, and Love to us, have been in a *then* advising, if he had been Equally poised. But this his partiality, may make some suspect that all this kindness for the first Commission, is but a meer *Shooing horn* to his designs by the second: and that he Loves *Massachusetts,* and *Connecticut* much alike.

6. What is fit, in answer to this *Pamphlet,* to be said why we gave such an Answer, as we did to this Commission, will occur afterwards, on account of the Commission of His *Excellency* of *York;* which being the contest with that writer, we do refer to what will follow.

PAM. In *Page 3d,* he begins, and so goes on, with an account of the like Commission of Leiutenancy, given by [12] Their Majesties to His ‖ Excellency *Col. Benjamin Fletcher;* and remarks upon it, *That upon notice hereof, the Freemen and Souldiers in the several Towns, are Convened; to see how they stood affected, and what they will Contribute, towards Addressing Their Majesties in this behalf. A General Assembly also is called and meets, and there it is resolved, forthwith to send an* Agent *for* England: *Money is provided &c.*

ANS. 1. And was not this Lawful and necessary? It hath been declared with sufficient Authority, *That it is the right of the Subject to Petition the King.* Let the *Bishops* case and what the *Convention Parliament* declared, be remembred; and might not in Lawful peaceable meetings, the Peoples minds be inquired into? and if they are found (as they were) so sensible of their concernment herein, that (in a manner) they Unanimously declare for an Address to Their Majesties, is it not thereupon just to take care for the Charges to defray it: and if this Unanimity and Vigorousness, grieve the *Pamphleter* and his *Abettors,* we are not therefore to be blamed. But this Arrow will not peirce, unless he head it. Wherefore he adds, as a part of that Courts Conclusion.

PAM. And Lastly, *That if any such Commission do come, in the mean time they will not submit to it, but oppose it, till they have answer from Their Majesties.*

ANS. 1. He seems to be very sensible, that all his labour will be lost, and his whole design (of Defaming *Connecticut*) frustrate, if he do not charge us with Explicit Resolves against their Majesties; and therefore if truth will not afford him matter for it; Lyes must and shall.

2. We say of this, as of the other Resolve, charged on us about the Commission to *Sir. William;* that it is a meer falsehood, forgery, our Records, and the whole Court are Witnesses of the contrary of it; and this, though for its truth, it could not have an *Imprimatur*, yet for its usefulness, it must be passed to the *Press.* It was said of old by *Cyprian, that some went abroad with Lyes, as if truth could not follow them.* And as one sayes of him that wrote the *Romish Legends; That he had an Iron Forehead.* So we may say of him, that Asserts as here a matter of Fact, which never had any being; and that of the Representative Body of the *Colony:* and to such perverse ends. The [13] Court Resolved ‖ or Concluded, only of an Address to Their Majesties, with what was necessary to it, as the charges, Person &c.

3. If these two great falsehoods, of the writer of that Book newly mentioned, and a third of Rising in Arms (which we shall meet with afterwards) be set aside, as they ought to be, for stark Lyes, that have not a Ragg of truth to Cover their Shame: all the rest affirmed against us (whither true or false) is too weak to bear the weight of his Reproaches cast on us.

PAM. *By these methods* (says he) *the Freemen of the Corporation, and as many of the People as will fall in with them, are ensnared, and strongly Preingaged, to make opposition against Their Majesties Commission.*

ANS. They engage only hereby in an Address; not in, or to, an Opposition.

PAM. *Insomuch that one Jeers, another will spend his Blood to keep off His Excellency &c.*

ANS. 1. There is not much (if any thing) to be believed on his Credit, nor his *Imprimaturs*, in this business; who have so departed from truth in what they affirm, and pass, of the General Court.

2. Though we have heard of no such speeches (from any persons of Credit) yet can we not say, but some Rude Persons, may have talked at this Rude Rate, and possibly on the as rude Provocations of some others. But still, is this fit to be used in reproach of a whole *Colony*, when yet none of the offenders were brought to any of the Majestrates, to answer such things? the particular Persons (if such they were) should have been named, and the evil confined to them: we take it as a wrong, to have these things indefinitely and Promiscuously cast on us, as if it were a common and general Practice; and hereon to ground in great part, the heavy imputations that follow. We shall oft meet with these kind of things: let this stand for an Answer to them, wherever they occur in the *Pamphlet.*

PAM. In *Page* 5, he gives an account of His Excellencies coming to *Hartford*, Reading his Commission, leaving a memorial of it &c. and in Particular, that he Assures us, *That he hath neither power, nor intent to invade our Civil Liberties: That in case of our Submission, he would Commissionate all that were in Commission before, and take our Advice for the* [14] *supply of Vacant Places. And particularly tender a Commission to our Governour, for the Command of the* Militia *in the* Colony; *only in Subordination to this* Their Majesties *Commission.*

ANS. We must defer the answer to this a little while, and see first his account of the Success of it, on the Court, in these words.

Viz.

PAM. *The Deputies (divers of them at least) being so prepared as aforesaid, are Resolved before hand, and have deter-*

mined the Question before the Court meets (God hath given them such a priviledge) and therefore if Their Majesties put such things upon them, they must oppose, and hold their own, they are bound in Conscience to do it.

ANS. 1. This Representation of the Deputies, as preresolved to Oppose Their Majesties Commission, is unlimited, and unproved, and therefore as here and afterwards improved, is an evil Surmise, and asperses all the Deputies, and the whole *Colony*, and opens a wide Door to any such Calumnies; but as long as it is wound up, to Resolving to oppose, it must be worthy of an *Imprimatur*.

2. The Court Act on this matter, shews what the Deputies minds were in it; and in honesty he should have produced that; and then they had spoken for them selves, and not out of the mouth of an Adversary. But that answer of the General Court, speakes not Opposition to Their Majesties, loud enough, he perceives, but Subjection; therefore in all his Book he recites it not, but in stead of it pops off his Readers with this Surmise, and other misaccountings of it.

PAM. *He then troubles himself with the* Halberteers; *as if they were designing to Conceal the Commission from being known &c.*

ANS. Tis a silly thing thus to imagine as he doth, why should any desire, or with what hopes endeavour a concealment? There were but four *Halberts*, and it was only to prevent a throng at first; the People were instantly admitted. But he adds.

PAM. *And no marvel the General Court not overwilling to give the Commission a hearing.*

ANS. This is another tacit Scandal cast on the General Court, who waited many dayes to give it an hearing (and this [15] our Records and ‖ the Printed account of those Transactions, Published by His Excellency do prove) and sate several dayes on it: and therefore for him to say, as he does on it; *That the Court take no great notice of His Excellency, wave the business, would bring him to Composition, as they had done* Sir. William *&c.* is apparently a mistake; we did take notice and attend as the account mentioned shews.

PAM. But he thought (it seems) that it would manifest Opposition to send, as he sayes, *Orders to such as Command the* Forts, *to prevent their Seizure.*

ANS. This misconstruction of Actions, is a frequent thing in this *Pamphlet.* The order he should have Printed, if there were any thing of an Opposition to His Excellency in it. The truth, and all of it is, That at that time, there was a *Pyrate* or Enemy on the Coast; that took many *Vessels ;* and it is usual with our General Courts, when they sit, to renew Orders of that kind, and that was what was then done : yet this is Rattled into the World, as a kind of Rebellion, and afterwards we are told of holding *Forts* against the King, wherein he seems to refer to this, but all that know our two poor *Forts,* may well Judge us all mad if we should attempt to hold them against the King.

PAM. He goes on saying, *And it seems (if the common Fame be true) it is their Opinion, That Their Majesties have nothing to do with us.*

ANS. 1. One would have thought that the *Topicks* of Lyes, evil Surmises, misrepresenting things, misconstruction of Actions, misapplications of Scriptures, and Laws; which are the *Nervous* parts of this *Pamphlet ;* had been enough to furnish the Railery of it, without taking in Fame, and wronging it too; for it may be truly answered, that unless this *Pamphlet,* by defaming, have so famed us, we never were so Reputed, in a common way, or at all as we know of.

2. What could he say worse of us, than that it is our General Courts Opinion (for of them he speaks) that Their Majesties have nothing to do with us? It is fitter indeed to be answered with renting our Cloaths in detestation, than with words. Do we not professedly and practically, hold all under Their Majesties? and Serve them to our Capacity as the rest of Their Subjects do? Say it be doubt-

ful as yet, in this one point of the Commissions? is all [16] Allegiance ‖ renounced, in one demur (on just Reasons as we trust) and about which we have (at great charge) sent with all speed to Their Majesties.

3. Let it be considered, what these his dealings with Their Majesties poor afflicted Subjects will prove; of his and his *Imprimaturs* Subjection to Their Majesties? however highly they word it for their Allegiance?

PAM. *He adds, in Page 6 & 7th. That hereon Commissions from His Excellency are declined, abuses offered him, and such of the Assembly as moved for Submission, thought unfit for their places; such as yeild obedience traduced as Rogues* (and with the rest) *yea some rise in Arms to Oppose him, and others are in readiness upon Occasion to do the same.*

ANS. 1. This of rising in Arms to oppose His Excellency here Asserted; is as false as any thing that can be told: that some came to *Hartford* with some Arms to list under His Excellency hath been said: but this cannot be the thing charged; also that some *Troopers* were appointed and went to wait on His Excellency to conduct him into *Hartford*, is true; but His Excellency came not at the time Expected, and they went no more. A Training was in hand but put by, by the Governours Order. Besides these (by all the enquiry we can make) no one man was in Arms in the *Colony*, while His Excellency was here: unless the *Halberteers* mentioned afore, and our usual Guards on the Lords Dayes; much less did any Rise against His Excellency, and least of all, yea not at all, as is here suggested to Strangers as a general thing.

2. This false charge, is by its confident Asserting, and Licensing past into the World; and down to Posterity, as a real truth.

3. We are by it greatly wronged, rendered (as the *Pamphleter* hath to effect his designs a necessity) as in open Rebellion. As to that of others being ready to Rise, it is only Surmised. The same we say of what was said of

some of the Members of the Court, being thought unfit for
their places; and the traducing of some as Rogues; and
abuses offered His Excellency; these things we have answered afore, that tis the particulars (if any such be) that
are blameable not the whole or body of the People. As to
the not taking Commissions, it will occur afterwards to be
spoken unto.

PAM. *In Page 7 & 8. Several things are said of a Proclamation, left with* Coll. Allyn, *imparted to the Governour,
and fault is found that it was not published, and so of a second
Proclamation sent from* York.

[17] ANS. 1. Let our General Courts Answer be considered; and that will shew how improper it was for our
Governour to Publish those Proclamations.

2. Was it not enough that no hindrance was given His
Excellency when here, and that he yet did not do it?

PAM. *In Page 8 he takes it for granted, that all former* Military *Commissions are Expressly determined, by the Publication of this: and therefore finds fault with* Trainings, *and
adds, 'tis said, we have made a* Major *too.*

ANS. 1. His Opinion differs from the General Courts,
in the first point, but that being Controversal, it is before
Their Majesties.

2. As to *Trainings* in the interim; it was it seems
thought meet by some Officers, not to desist, and thereby
let the Souldiers grow unfitted for Service, but attend what
the Law requires in a time of War as this is, here being
none in Commission neither, but what had Commissions
from the General Court; and a Vacancy at this juncture,
seems not safe.

3. As to a *Major;* the *Major Winthrop* being gone for
England, the General Care of *New-London* County, which
is most exposed to danger from the Sea, required somewhat of a Special Order in that respect. Our duty to Their
Majesties in our present Circumstances do admit, and require, that we omit nothing wherein we may best Serve

them. But these Trainings &c. in his usual heat he ill resents, and declares against.

Pam. *Thus we make all the defiance to Their Majesties, and Their Commission, trample them into the very dirt, and offend with as high an hand, as is well possible for us to do.*

Ans. It is time now to say somewhat more, to take of these heavy Imputations, and we will promise to do it; that there are several important things, that are not convenient on the Provocations of this *Pamphlet*, to be made Publick. Nor may a few, undertake to give the whole sense of the General Court and Country. We shall content our selves, and we hope satisfy the Reader, with what answers this *Pamphlet*.

1. Then we say, the *Militia* is the Kings. So says he in *Page* 25. and onwards.

2. This is so declared by two Acts of Parliament, 13 & 13*th*. and 14*th*. of *Charles II.* So saith he, *Page* 26.

3. The *Militia* that is the Kings, and so declared in those [18] Acts, is ‖ the *Militia* intended in the Commission to *Sir. William Phipps*, and now to His Excellency of *York:* So he Argues, *Page* 26. saying, *It is declared by two several Acts of Parliament, of 13. & 13. and 14. of* Charles II. *and of this His Majesty was pleased to put us in mind, by express mention of the first of these Statutes in the Commission to* Sir. William Phipps. And in *Page* 3. he calls the Commission to His Excellency of *York*, *a like Commission;* and argues in *Page* 26. and onward, *our duty to obey this Commission, by Vertue of those Acts.*

4. The latter of those Acts, do to determine the whole Regulation of the Kings *Militia*, in 36 Articles; according to which His Majesties *Leintenants*, we conceive must Execute their Office; this we think is indisputable, unless that Act be void, or vainly urged on us by our *Antagonist.* We desire that a special notice may be taken, that this Act of 13. & 14. of *Charles II.* is the Limit, and Boundary of the Kings *Militia*, as it is Committed to, and is to be Com-

manded by the Kings *Leiutenants*, as such: and that if this be plucked up. (1.) The very *Lieutenancy* is taken away, being as to Law founded only hereon. And (2.) That if the Kings *Leiutenants* as such, can claime, and Command a *Militia* as the Kings, beyond the measure of this Act, what shall stop them from Commanding, who when, and in what manner so ever they please? (3.) The word [*Militia*] as it relates to the King and His *Leiutenants*, is restrained to this Act, and does not take in all that strictly may be denominated [*Militia*] for in a large sence, *Corporations, Towns, Families*, yea single *Persons;* have, and may have, that Furniture for War, offending and defending, as their respective Capacities do require, and admit, that may be called truly and properly [their *Militia*] and yet neither the things so called, nor that name, shall incorporate them into the Kings *Militia;* and put them under His *Leiutenant.* (4.) That when the King makes His *Leiutenant*, that *Leiutenancy* is necessarily referred to this Law, and stands in Connexion to it; and all words and clauses, in the *Lieutenants* Commission, must be accommodated to the tenor and true intent of this Act; and not otherwise: for as it is *Leiutenancy*, so tis but *Leiutenancy*, and what *Leiutenancy* shall be, and how far extend, this Act provides; these things we refer to the Readers notice in this whole contest.

5. In the third Article or Paragraph, as *Wingate* renders it, is said that the Leiutenants &c. *May charge any, where their Estates be, with Horss, Horsman, and Arms, that have* 500 [19] Pound Per. Annum *in Possession,* ‖ *or* 6000 Pounds, *in Goods or Money besides furniture of their Houses, and so Proportionably: And any with a Foot Souldier and Arms, that have* 50 Pounds Per. Annum, *in Possession, or* 600 Pounds *in Goods or Money, other than Stock on the ground, and so Proportionably; they shall charge none to find both Horss and Foot in the same County.*

We need recite no more here, only in the close of the foregoing Paragraph: it is said, *And the said Leiutenants, and in their absence or otherwise by their directions, the deputy Leiutenants, or any two or more of them, may Exercise and Conduct the Persons so to be Armed &c. as is here after expressed.*

And in the 25. Article or Paragraph, we find to the same Effect. *Viz.* The *Leiutenant &c. May from time to time Lead, Train &c. all Persons Raised and Arrayed, according to the Act of* 13 *and* 14. *of* Charles *II.* Chap. 3. Here it seems very plain, (1.) What the Kings *Militia* is. *viz.* Persons of such Estates as are mentioned. (2.) That the Kings *Leiutenants* as such, and by Law have only those Persons of those Estates under their charge and power. As yet nothing is offered us to prove it otherwise.

6. There is no such *Militia* so constituted, yet formed in *Connecticut;* therefore no Subject or Object of such a *Leiutenancy,* yet formally Existing here; this is well enough known.

7. His *Excellency* nor *Sir. William,* ever went about forming such a *Militia* here, by and according to the 3*d.* 4*th.* 5*th.* and 10*th.* Articles or Paragraphs, of the said Acts of Parliament: therefore were not opposed in Executing their respective *Leiutenancies* according to the Acts referred to in their Commissions: and Consequently not opposed in their Commissions rightly understood and applyed; and as the *Pamphlet* argues for them.

8. The *Militia* of *Connecticut,* as now constituted by the General Court, by vertue of the Charter, and as our need requires; consists of all Males from 16 to 60 years of Age, some few, as *Majestrates, Ministers &c.* only excepted, be their Estates what they will.

These things being thus, the Question is whether the Kings *Militia* constituted, and to be Governed as by said Acts, or the Corporation *Militia,* of another constitution, and Government (and therefore so constituted because so to be Governed) be the Object of the *Leiutenancy?* the disputes of the *Pamphlet* run for the latter; but still wholly on grounds taken only from the former; but that will not

[20] hold : for what Their Majesties claime by Law (that is by those Acts) they surely Execute upon, according to the same Law, or Acts of Parliament. 'Tis an happy truth, that all the People are their Majesties, yet are not all by Act of Parliament from 16 to 60 years of Age (that is Males) His standing *Militia*.

If this had come to practice here and His Excellency had called all from 16 to 60 to the duty of Souldiers, and they had refused as not having Estates to Oblige them by the Laws, his Commission is dependent on and must be exercised by; and the Corporation *Militia* strictly so called, had been severed there from; what a poor posture had that been in? when it may be the *Colony* would not have yielded an Hundred Souldiers to that part, it may be not half an hundred?

But it may be said, doth not the Commission say; the *Militia* of *Connecticut*, all the *Forces &c.* And this answers all. We say no: For we know His Majesty Governs by the Laws of the Realm; and this our Adversary not only yields us, but makes it the *Basis* of all his Arguing, in *Page* 23. where he saith, *In this case, (Rex præcipit & Lex præcipit) the Kings Commands and the Laws Commands, is all one.* So that by his own account the Laws Command and the Kings Command in the case are Mutual, and Reciprocal and do expound each other; that is the Statute of 13 & 13 and 14 of *Charles II.* do expound this Commission of *Leintenancy*, and all others of that kind and in the sence and under the Limitations of those Acts, it is to be taken and not otherwise. And this alone with the Consideration of the Constitution of *Connecticut Militia*, at once overthrows utterly his whole *Hypothesis* in the *Pamphlet.* And he might have spared the labour of all his *Sophistications*, in arguing and concluding as he doth from the one to the other, when as not the same thing, or a thing of the same Constitution is in both.

And here we must note his misrepresentation of those

Statutes as intending a *Militia*, which they do not by applying them directly to another kind of *Militia*, as he doth evidently all along. It is like he knew that they are but few Comparatively that Read those Laws, and yet fewer of his Readers that know or will be informed what a different *Militia* from that, *Connecticut Militia* is: and so the *Ambiguity* of the word *Militia* would not be discovered; and so it must and would be concluded, that if we hold any *Mili-* [21] *tia*, it was the same in the Statutes, ‖ (this is no fair dealing in him.) His Majesty claimes His right according to those Laws, and what is by Patent Granted to His Subjects, and is of another Constitution, we may be bold to hold that, till we can enquire His Majesties right and pleasure to be otherwise, and in this we claim not His Majesties *Militia*, as it is distinguished from, our Corporation *Militia*, it is all His Majesties in Service.

In a word, what is the Kings *Militia* so settled by the Laws of His Realm, we never gave the least hindrance unto His *Leiutenants* in: if they had claimed the Command of that and that only, and had been refused; some such Charges, as now we are laden with, might have had a colour, whereas now they have none. To a full management hereof, many other things should and might be added; but this may suffice to show that the *Pamphlet* by not distinguishing between *Militia* and *Militia*, runs into all manner of confusion; and chargeth us with claiming the Kings right, when we claim it not; but a distinct thing, and not that neither, but in Subjection to Their Majesties (what of the Kings *Militia* is involved in the Corporations we know not, till it be distinguished as the Law requires) if these things be not clear to others, they are so to us, and will bear at least an enquiry in *England*, before we be put on, to what we are not clear in; and this may be the better born with, since as he said in *Page 5th. His Excellency offered to continue the* Militia *in the hands it was then in*, which shewed a good Satisfaction in the *Military* Commission Officers; the odds of being under the Corporation, or His Excellency, till we could here from *England*, needed not the Sharpness of this *Pamphlet;* which hath nothing helped; save to render us as bad as possible, and beyond truth, or peace.

And here we might end our answer; but because of the long and bitter *Harrangue* that continues in that Book, and some things that must be cleared, we must attend it. And at once we will insert the Courts Answer to *Coll. Fletcher*, that all may see what it was, and not take it in the disguises that are put on it; and it shall be as it was Printed at *York*.   *Viz.*

To His Excellency Benjamin Fletcher, *Captain General, and Governour in Chief, of Their* Majesties Province *of* New-York *&c.*

IN Return to your Excellencies demands of the *Militia*, of us Their Majesties General Court of Their *Colony* of [22] *Connecticut:* we ‖ say: That finding in your Excellencies Commission no Express, *Superseding* of the Commission of the *Militia* in our *Charter*, nor Order to us from Their Majesties to Surrender the same: And being sensible of the great importance of this matter, and finding it in several main things which do need a particular Explication, and Settlement, as we shall (God willing) manifest to Their Majesties: cannot but conceive it our duty, both with respect to Their Majesties Service, and our own peace, and preservation in this time of War, to continue the *Militia* as formerly; till by our *Agent* now sent for *England*, we shall receive further Orders from Their Majesties.

And in obedience to Their Majesties Gracious Letter of *March* 3d. 1692. We shall be ready upon all just Occasions, to yield Assistance to His Excellency *Coll. Benjamin Fletcher* Esq. His Majesties *Captain General*, and *Governour of New York &c. and to the Commander their in Chief, for the time being:* for the defence of the said Province,

against the Common Enemy, according to our ability, and
in proportion with our Neighbouring *Colonies* and *Provinces;*
although we have already been out about *Five Thousand
Pounds,* for the defending our Neighbours of *Albany,* since
the War began, besides the loss of Lives. And further,
this Court does see reason to grant the Sum of *Six hundred
Pounds* in Country pay, out of our Country Rate, towards
the Charge of maintaining the Garrison at *Albany,* onwards
of what shall be our proportion of that charge, in Obedience to Their Majesties Letter of 3*d* of *March* last.

By Order of the Governour and General Court of Connecticut.
HARTFORD October,   *Signed by* JOHN ALLYN Secr.
25*th.* 1693.

On the 27*th. of October* 1693. *was sent this* Memorial *following.*
Excellent SIR.

WE have in our former to your *Excellency, tendred you
Six hundred Pounds, in Country pay out of our Rates;
towards the charge of maintaining the Garrison at* Albany, *onwards of what shall be our proportion of that charge.   We desire your Excellencies answer, whether that be acceptable to you.*
[23] *But if you judge it more for Their Majesties* ‖ *Service, to
have men, we shall raise about Fifty men to Assist in Garrison-
ing* Albany, *who we shall raise and send forth, with what speed
we may, to continue there till the Spring to the end of* March,
or first of April *next.   We Crave your Excellencies Answer,
who are,*

*Your Humble Servants the Governour and General
Court of* Connecticut.
By their Order signed JOHN ALLYN Secr.

HEre is what can be charged truly on our General
Court; and the Spirit of it is in that clause, where
it is said, *We cannot but conceive it our duty both with Respect
to Their Majesties Service, & our own Peace, and preservation in
this time of War, to continue the* Militia *as formerly, till by our*

Agent *now sent for* England, *we shall receive further Orders from Their* Majesties. And this is spoken only with respect to the Corporation *Militia*, not at all with respect to a Militia Constituted as by the 13 *and* 14 *of Charles II.* which for distinction we call the Kings Militia, and on the reasons there aleadged, the full import of which is for Their Majesties special Audience: and with a provision to do our duty as to aiding *York* and *Albany.* And what does this amount to but our Courts sence, Judgment, or Opinion, in the matter of their duty.

Let any man cooly Consider, whether this be not justifiable, whether this will bear all the Mountainous weights of Reproach, which this wretched *Pamphlet* casts on us on this account? And had the *Pamphleter* dealt with any honesty, he should have proved that for our Court thus to declare their sence is Opposing the King, and what else he loads us withal; and not publish Horrid Lyes of us, and then argue from them. We know that sins and vices are *Immergent* as well as Graces and Vertues. Lyes evil Surmises misconstructions and the like, will yield Misapplications of Scriptures and Laws, and these then will yield a torrent of *Infamy.* But had he derived only from truth, it had been otherwise then now it is, and better for him and us.

In Page 9, 10, 11. *He tells us of two sorts of People among us. Viz. The Deceivers and the Deceived, and compares the best of these to the Rebels on* Absoloms *side, and their case and danger like the Regicides, and adviseth them to take the course of* [24] Peter, *who had denied his Lord* ‖ *and* Master, *the other sort are desperate &c.*

Ans. 'Tis to much to Transcribe it, but the Reader that hath that *Pamphlet* may examine it.

1. He is over what is matter of Fact, as to the main of it; and this, and what follows, for the Substance being only his own sence of the things fore mentioned; we shall pass through them more briefly: And we shall once for all, de-

sire the Candid Reader to take notice; that all his loud Openings and Noise, are upon a wrong scent; for he pursues us as with-holders of the Kings *Militia*, settled by Parliament; when as but newly declared we meddle not with that, but another thing only.

2. It would and should make any one tremble, to read such things, such Comparisons made on such wrong grounds; but we would know not only the words, but the power of these men, thus to Arraign, Condemn, and Execute (as far as *Pen* and *Imprimatur* Malice can go) Their Majesties Subjects and the People of God. Surely if the double Fence of Sacred and Civil Laws, had been at all regarded, we had not been thus Broken in upon, and devoured in some of our choicest Interests: the Holy ninth Command in its several Branches by the things mentioned, and to be mentioned is by the *Pamphlet* Violated Lyes, Reproaches, evil Surmises, Misconstructions, Misrepresentations, and the like, do Violate that Rule. The fifth Command to *Honour Superiours, Equals, Inferiours &c.* Requires the hiding real Blemishes, not with *Ham* to see and deride, were that the case with us, much more it injoyns not to Invade our just Repute, with Falshoods. By the Civil Law we are Their Majesties Subjects, and as such his Honour is in a degree concerned in ours, and Sugestions against the Subjects ought to be made to the King, not to the World, to defame the Kings Subjects openly, in the Face of His Enemies, sorts with no Law or Policy: nothing is to be done in terrour of the People, the Kings Peace is to be kept by all, the King hath a Judicature to Issue Controversies, and our cause, is at *Cæsars* Judgment Seat where we ought to be judged: who made this man a *Censor* over us? But all these things notwithstanding to tear and worry us is what that wretched Tract seems designed to.

3. What Colour is there that we are with *Absoloms* Rebels pursuing Their Majesties, or with the *Regicides* about their work, or have we denyed with *Peter* our Lord and Master.

[25] 4. May we not for his thus Comparing us retort his own Interogations; and say, Consider how he by these carriages Blemishes Religion and Scandalizes the Gospel. *Hath he thus Learned Christ &c.?* The Tables thus turned would stand the righter way.

5. Our Gracious KING and QUEEN, nor any of Their good Subjects, we do believe do like a *Phalaris* with his Brazen *Bull* to Torment men in, to Extremity; which this *Pamphlet* is but too like unto.

6. The *Pamphlet* goes on, to tell of the Fountain of good Principles, and what his are, *Page* 12 to *p.* 21. We will give only the heads of them, and his Inferences from them against *Connecticut*.

PAM. 1. *That Allegiance to our Prince is a Morral and necessary Duty.*

2. *That Religion Comprizeth both Tables of the Law.*

3. *That the Second Table of the Law is like unto the First.*

4. *That the Morral Law is not abolished by Christ.*

5. (To abreviate it) *That the King is next to God Supream upon Earth, Chief Governour in all His Dominions.*

ANS. 1. The manner, and end of Exhibiting these *Principles*, is to Suggest, that we in *Connecticut* are *Hetero-dox* in these points, and so little distant from meer *Infidels*: this perverse Insinuation we detest.

2. We own, and desire to live by these Principles, though we are yet so unhappy, as not fully to understand our duty in the one point Controverted.

3. Therefore all the pains taken in these 11 *Pages*, may justly be called, The *New-labour-in-vain;* a washing a white man, as if he were a black-more, to make him white, when as he never was other-wise.

PAM. But he infers on the first Principle, *that now it seems this Sound Doctrine will not be indured,* Page 15*th.*

ANS. 1. When or wherein was the Doctrine of Allegiance to our Prince, so Opposed or Punished among us, as not to be indured? The present contest turns not on that hinge, whether we shall be Subject to Their Majesties, but what is the true intent of this Commission? this we may enquire without renouncing our Allegiance.

[26] 2. Since the 40 years mentioned, it is well known who Preached an Election Sermon, on *Rom.* 13. 7. *Honour to whom Honour;* and how well he Prest Obedience to the *Colony* Government thence, and it were well if some were still as willing to be minded of their duty to God, and their Brethren, as the body of this People are to be Subject to Their Majesties.

PAM. On the Second Principle, *Page* 17. he sayes, *But we have seen that of late in* Connecticut, *which if* Abraham *himself had been here, would have made him say as once he did to* Abimelech, *because I thought surely the Fear of God is not in this place.*

ANS. This is like the most of the *Pamphlet,* a bitter Censure, and Causless; and we doubt not but he hath deeply wronged therein, many a Son of *Abraham.*

PAM. On the Third, he glances on the *Pastors* of the Churches, *and I may add, then, and not before will* Religion *too be sound and safe, when Obedience due to* Princes, *shall be thought to be a part of* Piety; *and when the* Pastors *of the Church shall Train up the People by the* Word *of* God, *to perform Obedience to them.*

ANS. The Emphasis seem to lie in the word [*then*] whether the meaning be not that it is not so [*now*] or as yet, we refer, but these Persons he is aware of, and therefore comes so on, as he may Retreat.

PAM. On the Fourth Principle thus, *That a Godly Rebel is a* Scolecism, *a Prodigious Monster in Religion.*

ANS. Who this is spoken to, and of, is Obvious: and what he bated the Reverend *Pastors,* he give in over weight to their *Flocks,* and but that some *Tongues are unruly Evils full of deadly Poison,* it would not have been thought, that such Reflections should have been made on us.

PAM. On the Fifth, *If our Religion be so over grown,*

to that pass that it teaches us to deny Kings *and* Majestrates *&c.*

[27] ANS. Is it not too much that our *Civil* and *Military* benefits, have been so struck at by some, but must our *Profession of Religion* be also prostituted to Contempt in this manner? We profess no Religion that teaches to deny *Kings* and *Majestrates :* but of this enough before. Yet we would tell the *Pamphleter,* that he is Suspected of other Principles, such as afforded all the untruths and *Ranchors* of his Book; and that *Leven* hath spoyled the use of these his Principles herein; and however high his Credit hath run abroad, and formerly, we will here tell him: that it is no good Principle for any to hold, that a man may Lawfully Marry with his Deceased Wives natural Sister :* nor no good Practice to write a Book to justify one that hath so done; which its said will be Printed; this is contrary not only to the Current of Protestant *Divines,* but even of *Papist;* and the *Pope* himself, save as he holds that he can dispense with the Law of God for the good of the Church, and the Manuscript is now extant to prove this.

PAM. *In Page* 20 He resumes what he said of us from Fame, *Viz. That it is our Opinion, that the King hath nothing to do with us; and thereupon proceeds to prove that His Majesty hath to do with us, as if this last were a denyed, or doubted Principle with us.*

ANS. It is too long to Transcribe, for it begins in *Page* 20. and ends in *Page* 25.

1. But it is *Coincident* with that aleadged opinion as (represented by him, by us denyed) and also with his fifth Principle but now answered; and therefore we need here only

---

* In May 1694, Nathaniel Finch was complained of before the Court of Assistants for having married Elizabeth Hemminway, the sister of his first wife; the court "having considered the matter of the complaint, with all the circumstances of the case, the pleas on both sides, and likewise the rules of God's Word, the judgment of most able Divines, and the Laws of this Colony," unanimously judged the marriage incestuous and unlawful, and declared it to be wholly null and void,   C. J. II.

say what in effect we have said; namely that it is a falsity, and figment of his own, to say and insinuate that we deny Their Majesties Authority over us, and therefore all his Interogations, and wretched conclusions on that Suppositions of our denying Their Majesties we detest, and if he will go on with a *Labour in vain* (unless it be to wrong us in the highest) he must, we can but Vindicate our selves.

2. We can tell him, that the highest word Assertors of Soveranty, are not alwayes the truest Subjects: *Haman* under the pretence of exalting and benifiting his King, sought his own Revenge, and used the Royal Bow to shoot down good Subjects: And no Age has been free of this Pestiferous mischief, when Subjects are leveled at, while they are on their Knees before their King, as now we are; [28] it is no great ‖ Indication of Obedience to Their Majesties, or Love to Their Subjects.

PAM. In Page 22 he saith: *It is a manifest thing, that this and the other* Homunculus *hath a thousand times more Authority, Respect, and Obedience in* Connecticut *than Their Majesties have. If a man come in Their Majesties Name, and with Their Commission, he will not be received by us; but if a man come in his own name without Their Majesties Authority and Commission, him we will receive: This is not the behaviour of good Subjects.*

ANS. Either this is a base Reflection on those worthy Persons of the Neighbouring Jurisdiction with whom we have for the Publick been concerned (it can intend no other) for who have we received *Viz.* Aided but his Excellency of the *Massachusetts*, and before him the Administrators of that Government, and those of *Albany* and *York* at the Instance of them and by the advice of the *Massachusetts*, to call these as he will have it *Homunculus;* we received also Mr. *Livingstone* of *Albany* when Mr. *Leisler* vexed him; these were the *Homunculus* the little men we received, but not in their own names, it was only to serve the Publick; or else we are here taxed as if we used Their Majesties Authority

9

to serve private Persons and Interests, which is a gross Slander: he should have named some of the [*Homunculus*] that we received in their own names and preferred before Their Majesties, that our answer might have reached it particularly; as for Mr. *Leisler* it will be spoken to afterwards.

PAM. *In Page* 25 *he moves us an Objection as made by us about the Lawfulness of* Coll. Fletchers *Commission, and this he returns over into an Asserting the Kings Right in the* Militia.

ANS. 1. As to Their Majesties right in the *Militia*, it hath been owned, and that he may grant Commissions accordingly is not to be doubted. But this is not the difficulty, but whether this Commission do reach any other *Militia* than what the Laws of the Realm do constitute, and this the *Pamphlet* in words at least yields in our sence, for in *Page* 29. thus he saith, *This Commission is therefore a Lawful Commission being founded upon the Antient and standing Laws of the Realm.*

If then there be an Inseparable Connection between this Commission and the standing Laws of the Realm, and it be [29] founded on ‖ them, and that Act of 13 & 14 *of Charles II.* be such a standing Law? then this Commission is measured and limited by that Law, which extent of it, was never denyed that we know of. But (2.) If they will extend it to a *Militia* of another Constitution, *Viz.* The *Corporation Constitution;* then there is matter of Law in it, not only to be disputed, but to be tryed, or at least to be inquired of Their Majesties, whether it be Lawful or no in that Extent. (3.) Their Majesties pleasure may be sought, even as to that which the said Act (if applyed) would take out of our Constitution of the *Militia;* wherein many things may be, and we hope are said before them. (4.) If men that have neither 50 *Pound Starling Per. Annum*, nor 600 *Starl.* in Money or Goods (as most with us are such) shall refuse the duty of a Souldier in the standing *Militia*, what Law that this Commission is dependant on, will condemn them for so doing? and this as has been hinted will be our case; if the *Colony Militia* (so to call it which is the Kings too in a sence) be disolved; but of this we gave an account before; yet could not well omit this further notice of it.

PAM. In Page 31. he reflects on the Government as Severe and Sharp, *Upon any disacknowledgment of our disputable Authority. How Bragg and Peremptory should we have been if this Commission, in terminis had been given to us? Certainly* Fire and Faggot, *or the Noose of an* Halter, *had been good enough for any one that should have offered to oppose it &c.*

ANS. 1. Himself sayes, that Male contents never want Complaints and Commends a throughness in Government. *Page* 54. *p.* 58.

2. It is the general complaint, that *Connecticut* Government is too Mild; and possible those that know it best, will laugh most at this. Imagination of *Fire* and *Faggot,* and the noose of an *Halter.* What error is in *Connecticut,* in these things, lies on the other hand.

PAM. *In* 31 *and* 32 *Page, he speaks of Greedy catching at the Kings Letter of* 3. *of* March *last.*

ANS. This Their Majestics Letter was very Graciously sent, and we hope thankfully and dutifully received and obeyed by us; and he needed not speak so of it as Greedily catching; but we know to whom that Letter hath been an Eye sore.

[30] PAM. *In Pag.* 32, 33, 34. he charges Ingratitude to Their Majesties on so hard, that it is intolerable. It was an old Saying: *Say I am Ingrateful and say any thing;* but the best of it is, he is no fit Judge of any thing concerning *Connecticut,* who is thus Fire hot against us with Rage; and we have Their Majesties and moderate Persons to judge herein; we acknowledg (and wish we could do it better) Their Majesties kindness to us, and were it not transcendent, as the Sky is above the Earth, to this mans Spirit; we were very Miserable. But whether he be within bounds of truth, Sobriety, or Charity, let any one Judge; when he saith, *Shall we requite Love with Hatred, Tender Bowels with*

Malignity? for what else can our behaviour signify, but a Malignant Spirit and Inveterat Hatred, against the King as King, and who ever comes from him as such? We have sufficiently declared our Affections to the King, and what we should have done if we had Him in our hands; we should soon Rid the World of Kings, if we had them in our Power; Remember Hazael, Is thy Servant a Dog, sayes he, that he should do this great (i. e. *this abominable*) *thing? Yea, but when Temptation and Oppertunity met together, he did it notwithstanding, and verily so should we.*

Ans. This is such a Charge as shows the *Pamphleters* Spirit, in Lively and yet blackest Colours. To take the Altitude of this *Promontory;* this Charge or Surmise: Let it be considered. (1.) That to Imagine the Death of the King, is by Law High Treason. (2.) To Imagine the Death of Kings in General is yet higher or highest Treason. (3.) That such Imaginings are Sins of the most heinous nature before God. (4.) That such a People so Spirited are justly to be abhorred of all man-kind. Wherefore to Tax a *Colony* with such Treasons and Impiety, to render them an abhorance to all men, is so abhorredly Injurious to them, That if *Cerberus* had been brought to Bark at us, it is not imaginable he could more Hellishly have performed this task. Let *Leviticus* 19. 16. Be here again remembred, *Thou shalt not walk about with Tales among thy People: Thou shalt not stand against the Blood of thy Neighbour: I am the Lord.* We will set against it the mind of Excellent *Owen*, in his Book of the Dispenssing of the Holy Spirit *Fol.* 517. *Where Truth is not universally Observed, according to the utmost watchfulness of Sincerity and Love, there all other Marks and Tokens of the Image of God in any Persons, are not only* [31] *Sulied but ‖ defaced, and the Representation of Satan is most prevalent.*

Pam. *In Page* 34, he demands an Example of us, *who so ingratful who so disobedient as we &c.*

Ans. Supposing us to be such as he just afore affirms

us to be, we think none are like us or should be so, nor do we know any like him for misusing the Kings Subjects, in such an horrid degree.

2. But if the meaning be, who ever did Address a King before, they obeyed an Order they had to inquire further on (which only is pertinent here) as we have done Examples in a greater Latitude then that abound everywhere. For one let *Dan.* 2, 24, 25, Compared with the 13, 14, 15, 16, *Verses* be seen; Scores might easily be produced, that have acceptably done this, as well as we.

PAM. *In Page* 35, he thus Interogates us, *What? do we indeed intend to fall off to the* French &c.

ANS. When men are thus forming and feeding *Chymeraes*, it is endless and in vain to follow them; We are not falling to the *French*, nor from the King, and yet for diversion we will tell him that his Counsel [*If we intend so to do let us speak out*] is very weak.

PAM. *In Page* 36 *he urges us with the unseasonableness of our Acting, from the time in which we are Addressing Their Majesties, and with his usual Severity.*

ANS. If we should for once gratifie his humor, and say we mist it therein, yet what is he better than *Esops Doctor* to the Dead man? the case was sent away to *England*, and that before he wrote, and he is too late to help it.

PAM. *In Page* 36, *he grows Jocous, and tis all that he is pleasant in, in the whole Book, and but sour there too, he* Masquerades, *tells us that our Great Champion, our* Goliah *leaves us in the Lurch, the Stone is Sunk in his forhead &c. And shall we yet harden our selves &c.*

ANS. He uses a great Liberty, we know none that have so Lurched us, though the Stone of a Slander, that one [32] took a great Bribe at *York* ‖ has been cast at one of us; but its most like to be found in another forehead.

PAM. *In Page* 37, *he propounds the Event to Consideration, and this he Predicts will be* (1.) *That Friends will be ashamed of us, Enemies will Insult.*

Ans. We think his Friends (if he have any wise ones) will be ashamed of him, for his Trifling, and abusive use of Sacred and Serious things; and that his and our Enemies will insult upon us with this weapon he hath so unadvisedly or maliciously, put into their hands.

Pam. His Second Prognostick is, *That the King and Councel expects better things of us.*

Ans. He is all along too bold to give the Kings sence: it has been said of a *Chancelour* in some cases, that *he that knew the* Chancelours *mind, knew the Kings mind;* but we have no assurance that this mans Perception is so deep.

Pam. His Third Presage is that, *That we Prejudice Their Majesties Interests, frustrate Their Intentions, defeat Their Counsels &c.*

Ans. 1. As we justly dislike his fore staling Their Majesties Judgment, so we do but a little fear it, though that be evidently designed by his Book, and he may move in his own Orb, and not Soar with his *Icarian* Wings so near the Sun; alass little thing why thus *Cheek* by *Jole*, with the Soveraign power? will he perform the thing through thee? We know a divine Sentence is in the Lips of the King, *and that our Judgement cometh forth from the Lord.*

2. Let it be remembred that we do take care of our duty in respect of the War, and are out great charge as hath been said.

We will pass over his fond Conceits in *Page* 39, of the *French* Concluding that, *they have* Connecticut *to Friend, at least in a posture of Neutrality;* and that of the *Maquaes* being put to go to the *French,* as Instances only of one that wants to Sleep; and that of the Commission as what we had before, with this Intimation; that *Connecticut* hath also the Kings Broad Seal for their Corporation *Militia.*

Pam. In *Page* 40, he falls afresh to rating at us, *Do we not know, That to Levy War against the King, is High Treason* [33] *&c. That an Actual ‖ Rebellion or Insurrection is a levying War against the King. That a gathering Forces for* *the Removal of Councellors Altering of Laws &c. is levying of War against the King.*   *That the holding a Fort or Castle by force of Arms against the King and His Power is a levying War against the King &c.*

Ans. 1. We must refer to what hath be said chiefly for answer to these things; to avoid vain and tedious Repetitions; but as these things are applyed unto us, we may say as *Nehemiah* to *Sanbalat* Chap. 6. v. 8. *There are no such things as though sayest, but thou feignest them out of thine own heart.*

2. Hath not *Connecticut* an uncondemned right to somewhat of a *Militia?* Why may we not in the reverss, charge as hard those that interupt us; especially considering that the General Government is (under Their Majesties) yet in the Corporations hand, to which particular Officers (though by Patent) one would think should stand in some Subordination.

But it may be said, that we mistake him; he doth not charge us with Treason, levying War against the King; he layes it only as a ground to argue from, as he doth.

Pam.   *What Construction then do we think it will have, If we shall be found to Rise in Arms against the Kings Lieutenant Publishing His Commission and Commanding Obedience unto it; and by Force and Arms, to with-hold the* Militia, *and all Forces by Sea and Land, and all Forts and places of strength, in a whole* Colony *or* Province, *from the King against His plain Commission Published under the great Seal?*

Ans. 1. The [*if*] that all this is propounded with, makes it like a wet *Eale,* hard to take any hold on, or how to use it; but he intends not to beat Air, but to strike us in these things; and because here he seems to clench most of his Coblery we say.

2. If he argue from the former of Treason &c. to this of our holding (which he will call with-holding) the *Militia,* that the latter is as great, as bad, as the former or worse;

then we did not mistake him; and indeed his sence Suites best his Scope in the whole Book. But,

[34] 3. If he argue from the greater to the lesser, there is no great force in it: for though it be Fellony to kill a Man, yet it is not so to kill a Fly; though a man may not Rob, yet he may stand a Tryal in Law, for what he hath held quietly a long time (on a good tenure) ere he Surrender; and if finally he should be Ejected, yet a Tryal is due to him, ere a delivery is due from him.

4. All along the *Pamphlet* beggs, and not proves the main question; for he still runs away with this, that our Charter now gives us no use of any *Militia* at all; and on that Supposition he builds in a manner all his discourse; but this we differ from him in, and take it our right to have Their Majesties, and the Laws descission in.

5. What if after all this his Scuffle to bring our heads within his halter; the Charter and his Excellencies Commission, should be found to refer to divers *Militia's*, the one to a Corporation *Militia*, as formed by the General Court to our necessity, and without which we are undone; and the other to the Kings *Militia*, according to the 13 and 14 of *Charles II.* Or, which is almost the same, that they should refer to the same *Militia*, in divers respects: Namely, the one to what of our *Militia* falls not within the verges of that Act forementioned, and the other to what of it that Act will on tryal, be found to Comprehend; will not this reconcile the Charter and Commission? Or what if the Law, or Their Majesties Grace, will firm our former and present Station in these things? these things are not only possible, but hopeful, and he might have staid his hand, and not have run out upon us as Traitors, as worse than *Turks* as dispisers of the King, as he doth, *Page* 40. 41.

6. A Contest with His Excellency, is not a Contest with the King; if *Ajax* and *Ulisses* strive for *Achiles* Armour, this makes neither an Enemy to *Achiles* nor the *Greeks:* if *Herod* and *Pilate* differ abut Jurisdiction, neither is hereby

a Rebel against *Cesar:* Are not Contests about Rights to particular Commands frequent in the Courts of Princes? And though but one can prevail, yet is not the other made a Traitor for holding what he had till a decission be. The [35] *Pamphlet* ‖ over charges, in saying (in a case thus Circumstanced) *That disobedience and Contempt offered to the Kings Ministers, redounds and is done to the King Himself* (for *Connecticut* is the Kings Minister also.)

PAM. But he is bold at all adventures, to affirm that besides, *other vile Indignities (not fit to be named) His Excellency is in danger of his very Life, such as assert their Allegiance and declare their Submission, run the same Hazard.*

ANS. This is not the first nor second time we have found him at the trade of Impudent Falsifying, as is before noted; His Excellency was with all freedom and safety among us, nor were his Servants or any hurt or assaulted in the least degree, that ever we heard of; true it is he lodging at a Publick house and Inn, there was a concourse of People of different perswasions, and that discourses, and disputes were many is without question, as there are on many Occasions; yet to raise such things to an hazard of His Excellencies Life, or others; is a false Inference; Can he say that any man shouldered a Gun, girt on a Sword, lift up so much as a Staff, or hand in such a way? we have a full account of the contrary, we are deeply injured therefore, thus to be represented to the World, as a Company of *Assasinates;* and he that gave his *Imprimatur* to this, had reason enough to known the Contrary.

PAM. In *Page* 42, thus he sayes, *Some may imagine they have found a Neat way to defeat the Kings Commission, they will not take Commissions from His Lieutenant themselves, but will also deter others &c. . . . . . What? do we think he is to be put off with our Scurvy little tricks &c.*

ANS. Here he finds he touches ground, for all this while he hath been but floating, and hath contended only with words of the Courts &c. but when as not withstanding that

Indeavours were used, to find persons to take Commissions, and such an universal adherence to what was settled by the Charter was found in the People, as that those proposals would not take, and that this gave a *Remora* to all present further proceedings: the Observation of this puts the *Pamphleter* into this Rage, and passionate Exclamation against (whom he knows best) perhaps he meanes the Governour first, and then the Court, as thus perswaded. But [36] this is a groundless Surmise; it was the set and Spirit of those to whom such Commissions were offered, and of the whole Country in a manner, which they were sensible of that stood in the way; and needed not the adjuvancy of any of the Court to perswade to it.

2. Since the proceedings stoped here, he might have spared most of his Labour in taxing the Court with opposing (as he will call it) that Commission, and laying its present Ineffectiveness there where it centred not. Let this be well noted, and it will ease most of the other difficulties that are urged against us: Since it is run aground here in our *Pamphleters* own account, though it rubbed else where.

3. Yet is there reason enough to believe, that those few that were asked to take Commission (and they were very few indeed by all we can learn) and that at a second third or forth hand way (which may clear the most, and those few too, of refusing) none did it, nor any others would do it, in the least unwillingness to Serve Their Majesties, (for Them they Serve with their present Commissions) but as well understanding their previledg and Interest, from which a *Pamphlet* has not moved them; and the general sence and set of the People, is an argument of more weight in this affair, then we shall now insist on.

4. Yet the this using their Liberty, doth not render their Obedience to Their Majesties Arbitrary neither; nor is it a putting Them off with Scurvy little tricks; it is but a waiting to have that made clear in their Alteration (if it must be so) which yet is doubtful it seems to some.

5. Nor will this not taking Commissions merrit Their Majesties displeasure, as he suggests, *Page* 43.

6. Nor is it a necessary Consequence from not taking the Commissions so offered (if any were) that such are like, *the Citizens in the Parable that hated their Lord and that would not have Him Reign over them* (Nor that therefore His Majesty should or will say) *Those mine Enemies that would not that I should Reign over them bring hither and Slay them before me*, as *p.* 43.

7. Nor yet that we and our posterity shall be ruined, be declared Rebels, put out of Protection, be shut out of Com-
[37] merce, be reduced by ‖ force, kept under a strong Garrison be sorely Fined, fetch over some to *England;* as he gives his judgment in his way *Page* 44.

We must confess these things though hard, are a great abatement of what went before, of being Slain; But they only signify and are Effects of an *Incendiary*, and Horrible prejudication, on weak grounds, without any Authority; and for a close he shews how loath he is, that these things (or some of them) should not befall us; in these words, *and it is a new sort of Grace if They (Their Majesties) do nothing.*

It may be thought this man hath forgot that he writes in the Reign, and within the dominions of Just and Gracious KING WILLIAM and QUEEN MARY.

Now at last we have the Fish that has all this while, and with all this Baiting and Angling for been sought, as the pray, brought out; and the white all these Arrows Aimed at; set open in *Page* 44, 45.

PAM. *Let all good Subjects then Consider, and as they would deliver themselves from the Common Guilt, so let them distinguish themselves, and make hast to yield their due Obedience. And as for the Rest, we may say Father forgive them they know not what they do.*

ANS. We believe it will not be found in any Instructions from Their Majesties, that Their Commission to His

Excellency should be forwarded in these turbulent wayes, moving for Commotions among Their Subjects, who are in Peace among themselves; Save this and a few more Male contents (and so on other grounds than this business) and we perswade our selves, that it will displease them and all good men that shall Consider it, that private Persons should over the heads of those that here Serve Their Majesties in the Government; thus bespeak the People of this Their *Colony:* make such distinctions between them, and especially that the Holy Scriptures, the Laws and Their Majesties name, have been put to such ill uses, as are every where obvious, and that the same should have an *Imprimatur* also.

2. What he means by due Obedience, is evident from his Scope; but if any should ask how, or in what way shall [38] we ‖ yield it, as the case now stands? he sayes nothing by way of direction, for if he had its most probable that the executing it, would openly have Violated Peace, and Order, to beget an ill affection therefore against the present dispensations in the Government, and so to make way for some other, seems to be the drift of all this ill taken pains with the People. But surely our Settlement, or changes, must or should come from Their Majesties; and not by these meanes.

What follows is only several *Objections* (most of which are his own, not ours) and his Answer to them, to which we will briefly *Reply.*

1. *Objection.*

The Militia is very well disposed of all ready; King Charles *the Second of happy memory, did by His* Charter *for Himself and His Successors, Grant it to us and our Successors, in the Year* 1662.

It is too much to Transcribe his whole answer, the Sum of it is, *First,* what we overween our Charter. *Secondly,* That the King knows our Charter, and how the *Militia* was disposed thereby. *Thirdly*, That the Charter never granted us a standing *Militia*. *Fourthly*, Nor to send men abroad. *Fifthly*, That what was granted was not to the General Court. *Sixthly*, Nor no places of Strength, Forts &c.

Ans. To all these things we need say no more, but that the clauses in our Charter, and those Equivalent, in the *Massachusetts* former Charter, and *Rhoad-Island* Charter, were always understood and practized upon, as Commissionating a standing *Militia*, and the Rule of it to be next the King, first in the General Court, and that we could aid our Neighbours, hold Forts &c. without which he had been undone in the *Indian* War, and in no safety at any time.

But the discussion of these points is large, and of little use here: where the dispute is confined to the Supposed Competition of our Charter, and His Excellencies Commission, for the *Militia*.

2. He reasons all the Charter granted is void, because *the* Militia *is a Jewel of the Crown not to be granted by the King from His Successors, it is like* Abishag &c.

[39] *Reply*. 1. We need not it is in vain, and therefore we will not here medle with that Question, how far in a Charter to a foreign Plantation a King may make a grant of the *Militia*, for and from His Successors; it is plain that such a grant there is; but we wave that here.

2. Yet we have before shewn, that the Kings *Militia* as settled by 13 and 13 and 14. of Charles II. is a distinct thing from the *Militia* as settled here; so that though the grant may not hold as to the former, against His Successors, yet it may as to the latter, as being no part of that undemissable Jewel of the Crown, as we suppose, and withal, that as yet is undistinguished in this *Colony*, from the other.

Pam. It is Answered by him in *Page* 47, *That our Succession was determined in* 1688. *So that we cannot talk of Succession or Successors, without some new grant.*

Reply. This indeed if it would hold does all the business at once, for our Charter is gone then, and we know who hath played on this String all along since that year. Tis a large field, we will enter it no further now, than to say that as Good Judgments as we could get in *England* or *New-England* are otherwise. Nor have Their Majesties so declared yet of it, but rather otherwise: but this is in *England* where we leave it.

His *II. Objection*, which he makes in our name, is,

But we Suspect that this Commission is a Cheat, because the King was in Flanders *at the Date of it.*

Ans. This is to put a Cheat upon the World, and an abuse upon us, to render us as thus Objecting, like much of what is already detected, begetting Brats and Fathering them on the body of the People, on whom he does reflect in his Promiscuous Charge; to Render us Odious and Rediculous; he claps a fools Coat on us, and then derides us in his Answers; but this is no disappointment to us whatever wrong it be, we could look for no better from a Per-[40] son so ingaging ‖ as he in this *Pamphlet*. He and his *Imprimatur* may be ashamed of such things. What if some few should quere at the rate of this Objection? Is it thereby a General Court or Colony Objection? the Court never in their answers, took it for other then a reality ; as is plain by the Printed account of those Transactions.

His *III. Objection.*

The King hath given us no command to Surrender the Militia *to His Excellency.*

This he slights as a poor Shift, *as if Their Majesties Commission to His Excellency to Command were not Command for us to Obey &c.*

Reply. It is one thing for a Command to come to the Objects of it immediately, and another for it to come to them by a *Medium* (as the Government is where under they are.) Again, tis one thing for a Command to come without a Competing Command, and another when tis otherwise. *Thirdly,* Its one thing for a Command to be clear and indisputable in its intent, and another thing where tis not so.

If this Command must influence. (1.) The General Court and by them the People; if withal the General Court have a power to the same Command, and these powers are not cleared from interfering, in such a case, and when these also are depending for Issue, we say a Commission to Command is not imediately a Command to Obey, till those incumbrances are removed.

2. We have cause to believe, that the not ruling our right in the *Militia,* nor giving Orders for Surrendering: was done by Their Majesties, to give us the opportunity of applying to Them, in reference to it, in both the Commissions, or else as well our power as *Sir* WILLIAM PHIPPS, we think had been determined expresly.

3. Common reason suggests, that every one in trust, is to mind his own Orders, and Instances of this are plentifully discourst.

4. A Charter Grant is of that nature, that (so far as it is good) we think a particular Order does not null it, wherefore we lay not the stress of this matter chiefly there.

PAM. He sayes, *His Excellency Demands no Surrender of the* Militia: *But Obedience to His Commission, &c.*

[41] *Reply.* We ask, what was that Obedience he demanded of our General Court? or what Obedience were they Capable of herein as a General Court but a Surrender? Or why is our Court so faulted with opposition and disobedience all along; if they were capable of no Surrender? or had no demand thereof as here he saith? by this account their Audience, of the Commission, and not actually resisting his Executing it; was our Complyance, and discharge, and this he had to the full; and yet complanes.

PAM. The last part of his answer to this Objection, stands thus, *Did Their Majesties ever give Their Subjects any Command to yield Obedience to our resumed power? We lately*

*received a Letter from Their Majesties; did Their Majesties
therein or any otherwise give the People any imediate and
express Command to obey us, in what we were thereupon
about to do? Yet we expect Obedience from them, without
any such Command, and are not we Their Majesties Subjects
as well as the rest of the People?*

Reply. This is a poor shift indeed: Is it reasonable or
possible that every Individual Subject, in his private capacity, should have His Majesties particular command; as
it is reasonable and possible, that a Body Politick or Publick Person should? Every Inferiour is to attend the Orders of his Superiour, but Their Majesties are our Superiours, we may expect Their Orders therefore, though our
Inferiours must take up with ours.

His *IV. Objection.*

But we cannot manage our Government without the Militia.

Ans. This Objection is of great weight, and requires a
large Consideration to handle it, but its to no purpose here
to insist on it; only this is the general sence, that if all
Militia be taken from us, the Civil part of the Government
will be extreamly weakened, if not desolated thereby;
things in this respect are not here as in *England,* as might
be demonstrated if that were here to be done. The hith-
erto constant Conjoying of the *Civil* and *Military* power in
the foreign Plantations, is evidence enough of the necessity
of the one to the other. What is a Body without some
what defensive and offensive, but a prey, or at anothers
Arbitriment?

[42] His *V. Objection.* Is *Coincident* with the former,
only he adds somewhat about our annexing to *York.*

Reply. We shall wave this for the most of it, as being
no present inquiry whether it be good for us to be annexed
to *York?* that is not our business; and though he speak
of it as indifferent, or desireable, yet our People tis well
known desire their old Station.

2. Whereas some mention is made there, of our aiding *Leisler*, which some may take in a wrong sence; we say that what we did therein, was only out of a sincere respect to Their Majesties, at the Solicitation of *Albany*, and of *Massachusetts;* and it is known that Persons of Honour came from *Massachusetts*, and one from *Plymouth*, and joyned with our Agents there, in that matter; and the State of that Province, and of affairs in general needed it, and it was not out of any sinister or personal respect to Mr. *Leister*.

3. His Suppositions of our Shouldering out the Kings Government, which he insists on, are meer Imaginations of his own, without any ground given to it by us.

His *VI. Objection* about *Rates* are impertinent; and the complaints of the *Long-Islanders*, though loud, is not our business; unless it be to wish that others espoused no more the complaints of Male contents here, than we do theirs, who they give that name to there.

His *VII. Objection.*

That the Governour of York *is a Proud Moross Stearn and Austeer Man &c.*   And His *VIII. Objection, That he is a* Papist.

Reply. We say to these in Sum, what we said to his second *Objection;* Let the Reader turn to it, and when these are not our *Objections*, 'tis hard to be falsly taxed and thereupon to be further reproached as there; *Viz. Who knows when the* Devil *and his Children, will have done Lying and Slandering....*(and calls us) *a Rude, Proud, Ungoverned, Disorderly People, as we have declared ourselves to be:* And more to that effect as there it follows.

Reply. If these his dealings with our Colony be not [43] Rude, Proud, ‖ Ungoverned and Disorderly, we think never any such will be found in *Paper* and *Ink.* As to what *Encomiums* he is pleased to give His Excellency, we need to say nothing of it.

10

PAM.   For a farewell, and as the Sum of all, to give our Caracter as we stand in his account, he cites at large, I *Sam*. 10. 26. 27. *There went with* Saul *a Band of men whose hearts God had touched, but the Children of* Belial *said, How shall this man save us? and they dispised him &c. But he held his Peace.*

Reply.   Who these Comparisons intend is notorious; we have only this kindness from him therein; that he tells not the World how small a number that Band he aludes to, was; for then in all probability, it would have been known that he had called almost all the men in *Connecticut Colony*, Children of *Belial:* And there is one thing in it, that is Extreamly and to Admiration strange, and that is; that since his *Saul* was so wise as to hold his Peace, that he (one of his followers) should be so very foolish, as to write so much (and in the manner as he hath) about it.

PAM.   Lastly, he cites *John* 1. 46.   Nathaniel *said can any good come out of* Nazareth?   Philip *sayes to him, come and see.*

Reply.   We leave it to the Sober and Pious, whether he did not begin, go on, and hath not ended in a dreadful prophanness; Contrary to the *Third* Commandment, which enjoyns the true and Reverend use of the Holy Scriptures.

FINIS.